ME AND MY
MAMMOTH

Albury  Books

This edition published in 2020 in
association with Crane Press

First published in 2018
by Albury Books
Albury Court, OX9 2LP, United Kingdom
www.AlburyBooks.com

A CIP catalogue record for this book
is available from the British Library

10 9 8 7 6 5 4 3 2 1
Printed in China

ME AND MY
MAMMOTH

illustrated by
Jack Brougham

written by
Beth Shoshan

This is me.
And this is my Mammoth.

My Mammoth sleeps...
VERY deeply.

Where…
did THAT
come from?

So, what's inside?

Careful now…

Uh oh…

Let's play!

We can splish...

and splosh...

and stamp...

and **SPLASH!**

The water is rising!

Quick! Grab the box…

I wonder where we are going...?

...this way!

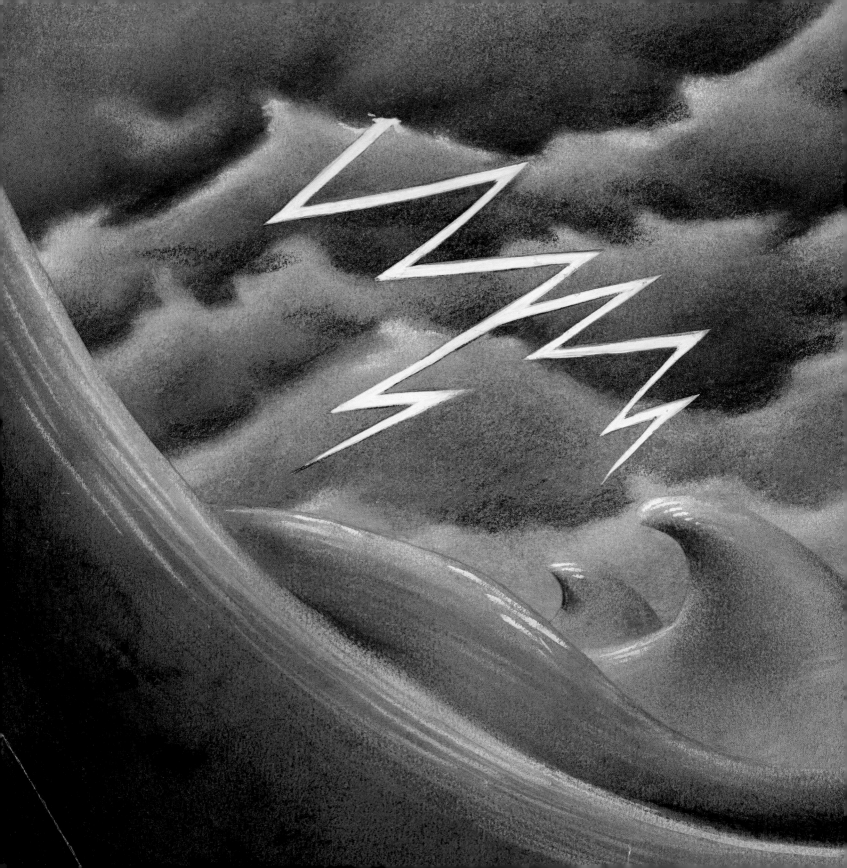

Watch out BELOW!

I wonder what else boxes can do...?